Self-published by Alasdair Hoswell 2019

Published by Alasdair Hoswell Publishing 2019

Written and Illustrated by Alasdair Hoswell 2019

Imagined and designed in Cornwall

First Published by Alasdair Hoswell Publishing 2019

ISBN: 9781077694415

For Manon, Tristan x Mathilda!

I hope you enjoy this book!

Alasdair Hoswell

I dedicate this book to all my family.

This book is also for my Nanny Dawe, Toby Joe, Michele Matthews and for dearest Julian Kitto, who loved a Cornish pasty!

To everyone who enjoyed my first book, this is for you!

Hello! My name is Alasdair Hoswell and I am a Cornish author and illustrator. I was born here in Cornwall and I love living in this beautiful land. I am also a primary school teacher - a job which I absolutely adore! Cornish pasties really are 'ansom, so if you haven't tried one hopefully my book won't put you off! I hope you enjoy this book and I wonder if you will spot any famous Cornish landmarks inside!

If you enjoyed this book, please tell me what you think. You can get in touch with me on Facebook- I'd be delighted to hear from you! @alasdairhoswell

Callum lives in sunny Cornwall, close to the sea. He likes to get up to mischief and he doesn't always like to do what he's told - in fact he likes to do the complete opposite, and this can get Callum into all sorts of trouble. It all began one day when his Nanny Dawe was visiting for the Summer Holidays.

Callum loved the Summer Holidays. He spent most of the time searching for precious pirate treasures on the beach at Penzance, looking for mermaids on St Michael's Mount and exploring Cornwall. Callum absolutely loved the beach - the best part was visiting the ice-cream man and eating all the different flavours of ice-cream, all at once! Callum had ten scoops piled on top of each other on a crispy cone.

“Strawberry, chocolate, vanilla, fudge, raspberry, bubble-gum, cookie-dough, lemon, mint and mango, all in my tummy,” giggled Callum, with a huge grin. But Callum’s favourite thing about the Summer Holidays was spending time with his Nanny Dawe. His Nanny was like his best friend; they would do everything together. Callum was always on his best behaviour when he was with Nanny, apart from when Nanny wasn’t looking!

Callum and Nanny Dawe often visited the Cornish fishing town of Porthleven - with its beautiful harbour and the best sunsets. Together, they would always go crabbing on the harbourside, visit the gift shops and, if Callum was lucky, his Nanny would buy him a tasty treat.

Nanny Dawe always knew the best places to eat ice-cream and they would often sit by the clock-tower, watching the boats in the harbour and the surfers in the sea.

"We'd best get something for lunch my 'ansum," suggested Nanny Dawe.

"Lunch? I want ice-cream, cakes and a big strawberry milkshake!" Callum said quickly, whilst rubbing his tummy.

"Oh Callum! Maybe you can have one sweet treat, but only after something savoury," Nanny Dawe replied, while cleaning her smart, round glasses. "Oh, what shall we have today dear? A sausage roll followed by a cream tea? Oh I know, maybe a pasty?" smiled Nanny. Callum's face dropped and he suddenly looked really miserable.

"I don't like pasties! They're nasty pasties!"

Pay Here

Callum would never eat his vegetables, and he hated any foods that didn't look like ice-cream, cakes, sweets or chocolate!

"I'm not eating anything with vegetables in! I don't want a nasty pasty!" he snarled, folding his arms grumpily.

"Now, stop your grumpiness, mister! An 'ansum, tasty pasty, won't hurt 'ee! A pasty it is!" said Nanny Dawe firmly.

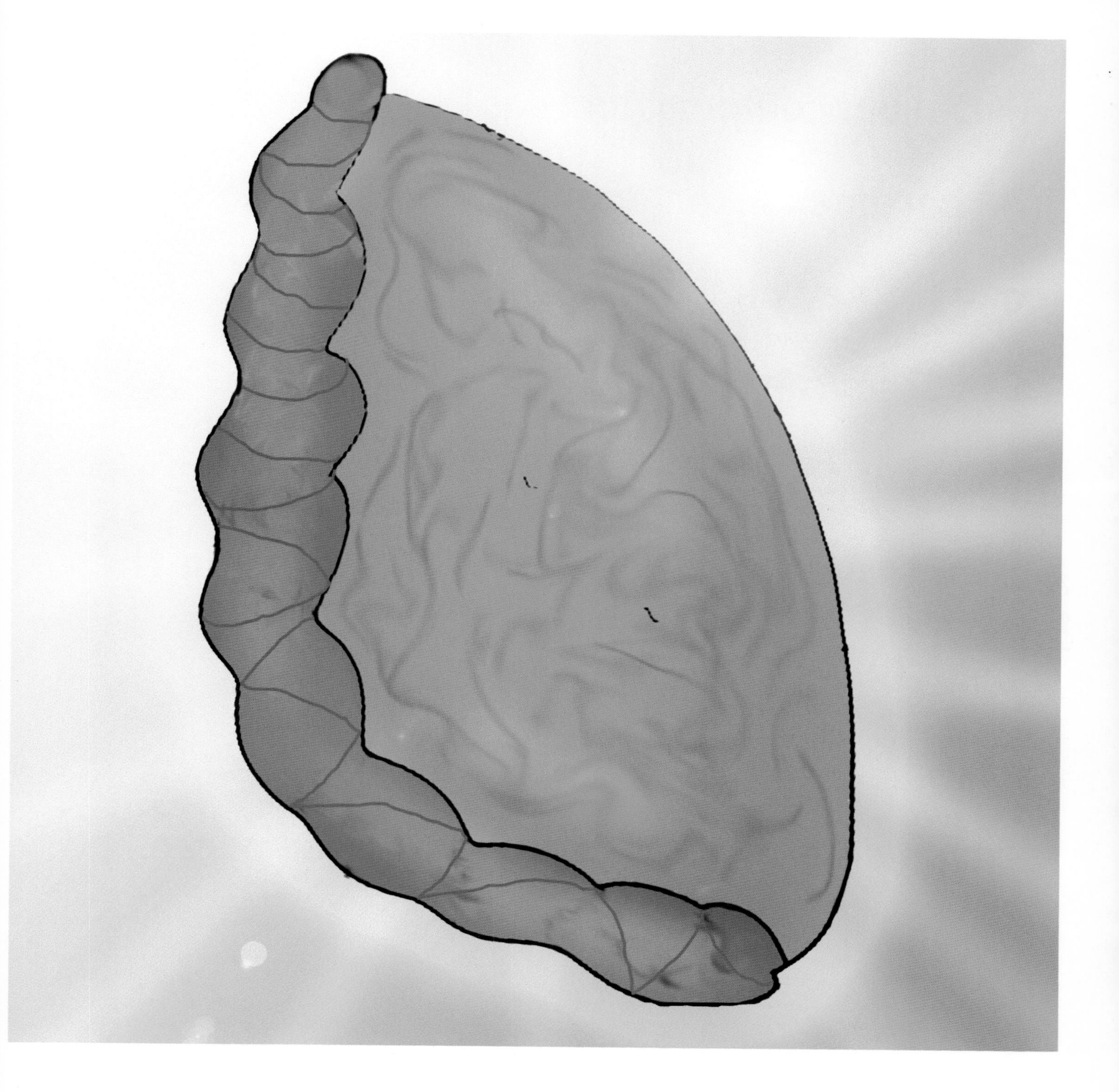

All Callum could notice was the sticky buns, the caramel slices and the fresh chocolate cakes. They all looked so delicious.

"Can I have two Cornish pasties please?" asked Nanny Dawe.

"Shortcrust or flaky, my love?" enquired the kind lady behind the till.

"Shortcrust please," replied Nanny, while searching around in her bag for her purse.

Nanny paid the lady and bought some

delicious looking pasties from the bakery.

They left the shop, with Callum's eyes still

glued to the sticky buns!

Callum was really grumpy as he didn't want a

pasty... he wanted the sticky buns.

Callum pulled the weighty pasty from the bag slowly, revealing its golden pastry.

'Yuck...this is a smelly-welly pasty with smelly-welly vegetables in it! I don't want to eat this pasty! I want the sticky buns!" he shouted.

"Callum, how do you know you don't like the pasty, if you don't try it?" asked Nanny Dawe.

All of a sudden, a sinister-looking seagull flew next to Callum, with a hungry look in its eye. The seagull was eagerly watching the pasty in Callum's hands.

"Oi! Go away, seagull! Go find your own food!"

Then, Callum had a sneaky thought.

"Oh! Wait a minute! If I get rid of this pasty, Nanny might buy me the sticky buns, the caramel slices and the cream cakes!"

Then, when nobody was looking, Callum threw his pasty towards the hungry seagull!

The seagull grabbed the pasty as fast as it could and flew off, before anyone could take it away.

Callum ran quickly to Nanny Dawe. "Nanny, Nanny, the seagull stole my pasty!" he announced, with a glint in his eye.

"Oh no!" sighed Nanny.

"Umm umm ... he snatched it from me!" Callum explained, while twiddling his thumbs. Of course, this wasn't the truth.

Nanny gave him a stern look ... the type only a Nanny could give.

"Oh no! Now I have nothing to eat for my lunch! I was really looking forward to that pasty," Callum fibbed.

"Callum, I hope you didn't throw your pasty to that seagull on purpose. Very well young man, we will go home and you can make what you think is the perfect pasty, that you would love to eat," suggested Nanny, with a crafty look.

"Alright! I'll show you how a proper Cornish pasty should be made!" promised Callum, rubbing his hands together.

Later that day, back at Nanny's house, Callum was playing in the upstairs bathroom.
He decided it would be fun to squirt his hair-gel all over the bathroom floor, as his space figures wanted to live on a sticky alien planet.
"Callum, it's time to make your perfect pasty!" shouted Nanny, from downstairs.
"Don't forget, we need to make your Dad's pasty too."

Hair Gel

Callum hurried down the stairs. “I don’t like the look of the ingredients: beef, potatoes and terrible turnip!” he said with his arms folded.

Salt
Pepper
Beef

“Come on my ‘ansum, you don’t have to use my ingredients. Why don’t you make the perfect pasty only Callum could eat!” suggested Nanny, opening the cupboards to reveal all the special treats that were hidden inside, making sure Callum could see them too.

“It’s your pasty, my love. You make it the way you want it to be,” she said with a knowing grin.

“Fine! If I have to make a pasty, I will make it the way I want to make it. It will taste scrumdiddleeumptious!” he said excitedly. Callum and his Nanny Dawe started to roll out the pastry together. “Right, we need to roll the pastry out - not too thick, mind, or too thin.” Nanny Dawe made the pastry just right.

"Oh, do you know what?" asked Nanny Dawe, "I've only gone and left my handbag in the car. I won't be a minute." Nanny Dawe left the kitchen, looking over her shoulder at Callum, smiling slyly.

Callum waited for Nanny to leave the kitchen, before opening the cupboard and grabbing the jelly-babies, chocolates and lemon drops!

Jam
Golden Syrup
Beans
Crisps
Flour
Sweets
Sugar
Salt

"I will add some jelly-babies to my pasty," he thought. "Oh, and I want lots of sugar in my pasty. What else do I need?"
Callum went to the fridge and found some Cornish clotted cream. "This has to go in my pasty!" Callum exclaimed. He then opened the other cupboard and found his favourite flavour of crisps... pickled onion Gremlin Grunchers.

milk
Juice
Juice
milk
Cornish clotted Cream

“Jelly-babies, clotted cream, crisps, chocolate, lemon drops and lots of sugar! The perfect pasty! Well, that’s my pasty sorted. Now, I need to make a pasty for Dad!”

"Dad will have the ultimate nasty pasty!" he said to himself, as he reached for the ingredients. Callum loves his dad, but sometimes Dad could be really bossy. Callum likes to have his own way, so to teach Dad a lesson, Callum decided it would be a good idea to make him a nasty pasty!

"Alright Toby Joe, let's make Dad the nastiest pasty ever!" Callum said to his dog. "Hmmm Dad can have a pasty with ..."

Callum went and found his smelly socks and squeezed the smelly sock juice onto the rolled out pastry of his dad's pasty. Callum laughed to himself!

"Smelly socks are yucky and really nasty, they can go inside the pasty!"

Callum opened the cat's cupboard ..."I think some cat biscuits would add some flavour," he sniggered. "Cat food is yucky and really nasty, it can go inside the pasty! Also, some toothpaste for minty freshness! Toothpaste is nasty when it is inside a pasty."

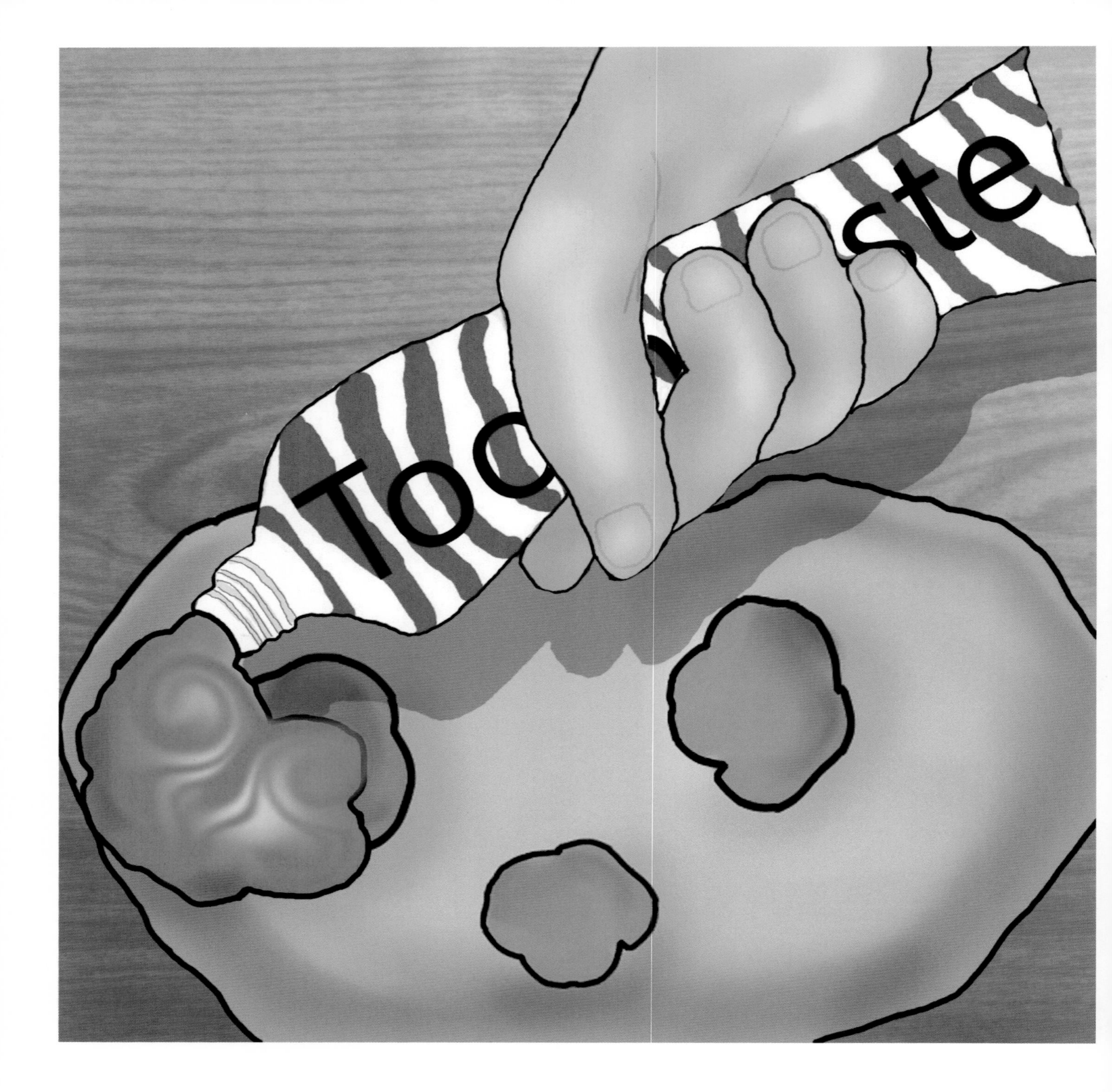

He then opened the fridge. "Yuck! Mum's leftover fish soup from last night- this will do! Fishy soup is yucky and really nasty, that can go inside the pasty!"

Callum wondered what else he could put in the pasty. "Carrots! Everyone knows a Cornish pasty should NEVER have carrots in it!" he chuckled loudly.

"Carrots are really nasty - they can go inside the pasty!"

Before Nanny could see what was inside, Callum pinched the corner of the pastry and folded it over. He pinched and pulled, tugged and pressed the pastry together, forming a perfect crimp, enclosing the secret ingredients within.

Just then, Nanny Dawe walked back into the kitchen. "Right my 'ansum, I've got the ingredients - all we need to make the perfect Cornish pasty: beef, onions, turnip, potatoes, salt and pepper, bit of butter, and a glaze of milk and egg."

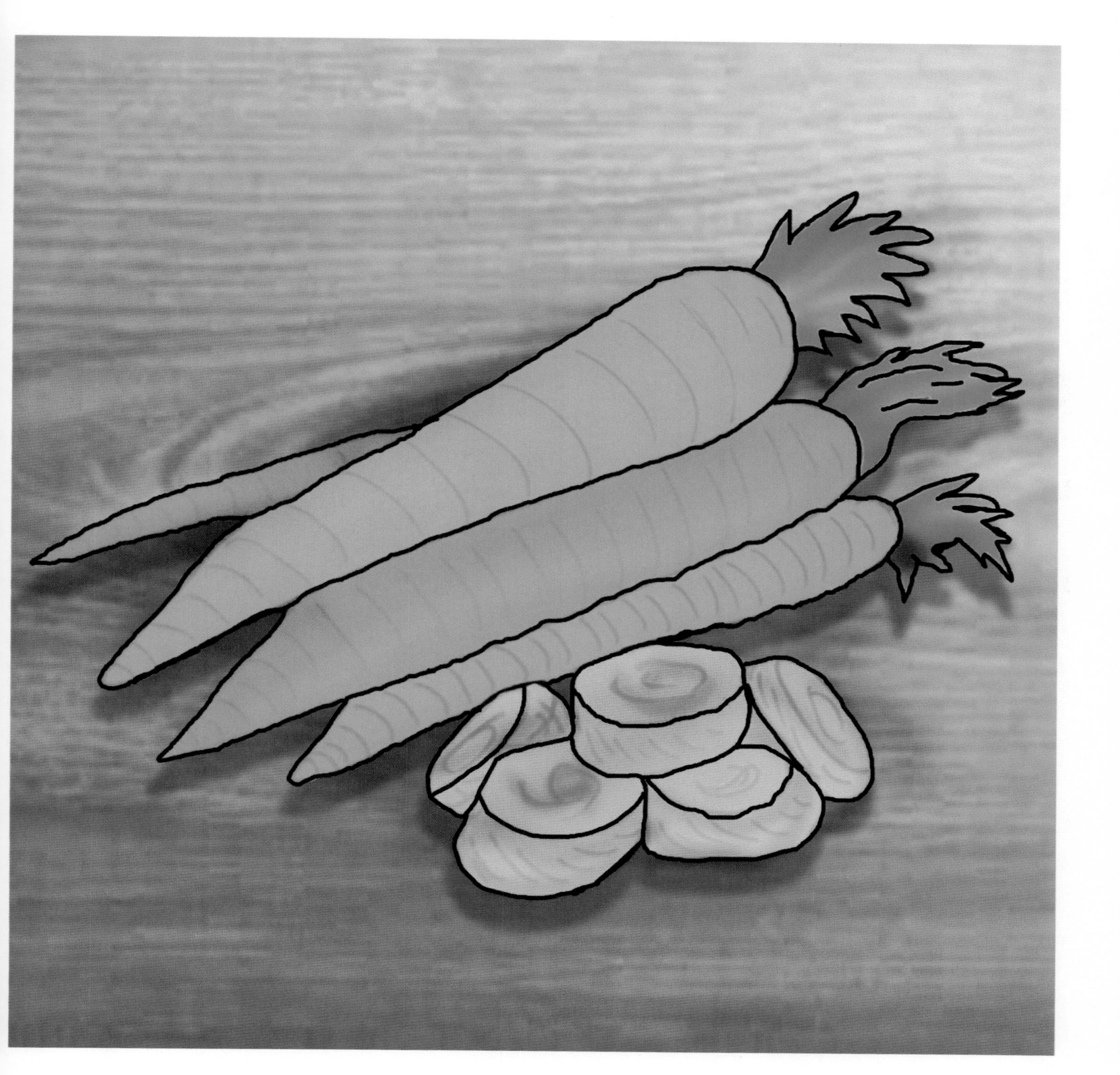

However, Callum knew differently. He knew the perfect pasty has much more exciting ingredients than that!

"No, it's not! It's sweets and chocolate and lovely things that I love to eat - not smelly vegetables," he whispered to his furry friend, Toby Joe.

How to make the perfect Cornish Pasty

Ingredients

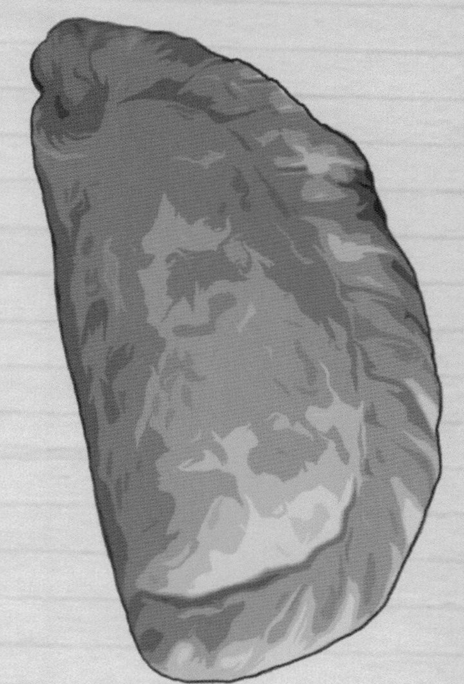

Quality beef skirt, cut into pieces

Turnip, peeled and sliced

Potato, peeled and sliced

Onion, peeled and sliced

Salt and Pepper

Knob of Butter

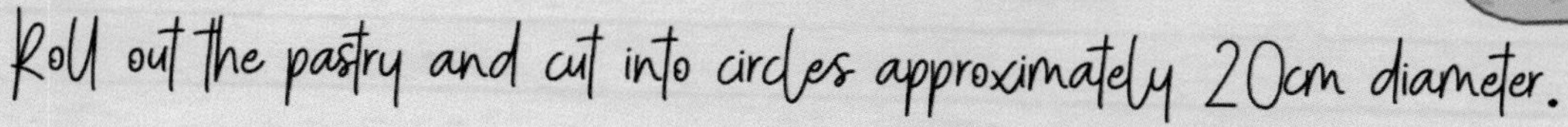

Roll out the pastry and cut into circles approximately 20cm diameter.

Layer the vegetables and meat on top of the pastry, adding salt and pepper.

Put a knob of butter on top and a sprinkle of flour.

Bring the pastry around and crimp the edges together.

Glaze with egg or milk.

Bake at 165 degrees C for 1 hour, until golden brown.

An hour or so later, Nanny Dawe called to Callum, "The pasties are almost cooked!" Just then, they heard the front door open.
"I'm back!" called Dad. "What a long day! I've been looking forward to my pasty all day!"
Callum laughed loudly.
"Oh Callum! Please pick your dinosaurs up off the floor. I almost fell over them!" shouted his dad.

Callum raced to see his dad. “We have been making pasties today and I made a really special one for you!” he said excitedly. Callum’s dad sat at the dinner table with the rest of the family, all ready to eat the delicious homemade pasties. Nanny Dawe placed the pasties in front of them.
“This is yours, Callum, I believe.” Nanny winked at Callum and placed a very plump pasty in front of him.

"It smells great!" he said. Little did Callum know, Nanny had switched the pasties when he wasn't looking. Nanny had an idea. "I think you should close your eyes when you eat your pasty, Callum." Callum thought that it sounded like fun, so he closed his eyes tightly.

He took a bite from the pasty. "Delicious! This is so good ... it must be the jelly-babies!"

He took another bite. "This is scrummy ... must be the chocolate!"

He took yet another bite. "Mmmmm - this must be the lemon drops ... this is such a tasty pasty!"

Within a few minutes, Callum's pasty was gone! He had eaten every last bit!

"Now, did you enjoy that pasty, Callum?" asked Nanny Dawe.

"Did I enjoy it? I loved it! There was nothing nasty in that pasty! It must have been all the sweets I put in it!" Callum sniggered.

"Sweets!" shouted Nanny. "Oh no! Dear boy, you mean the pasty you made earlier? I thought that was Dad's special pasty so I saved that back for him," explained Nanny Dawe.

"Oh what? That was my pasty! Hang on! Whose pasty did I eat then?" asked Callum, with a confused look.

"You had a traditional Cornish pasty, my 'ansum and it seems you enjoyed it after all!" Nanny Dawe laughed, wagging her finger.

Surprised, Callum asked, "You mean I have just eaten a real Cornish pasty? Oh … well it was actually very tasty, Nanny. I still think the sweetie one would taste better though! BUT WHAT ABOUT THE PASTY I MADE FOR DAD?" he shouted.

"I saved that pasty especially for you Callum, as I thought you enjoyed making it so much! It's smelling strong- you must have used some lot of onions, my boy!"

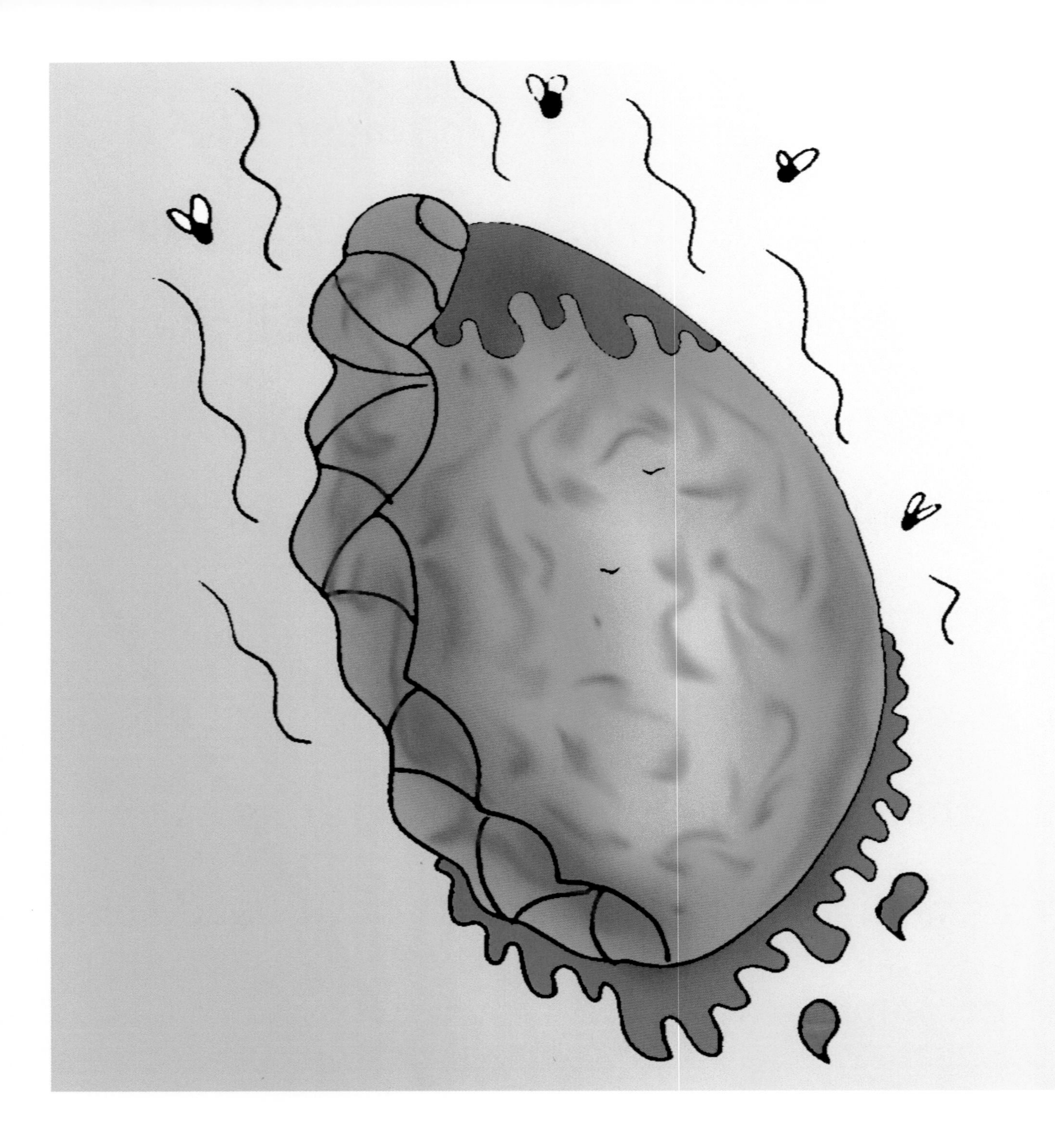

"Ah ok ... umm no, I don't want that one, thank you!" Callum replied, anxiously.

"Why not, Callum? After all, you made it yourself for Dad," asked his mum.

Nanny Dawe placed the pasty in front of Callum ... it was smelly and had oozing slime coming out from the bottom of the pasty, instead of gravy.

Nervously, Callum picked up his pasty and very slowly took a bite. It was oozing slime and smelt like fishy socks.

YUCK!

"THERE'S

SOMETHING NASTY

IN MY PASTY!"

shouted Callum, spitting the pasty back out!

"Yuck! Yuck! Yuck!"

Toby
TOBY

Later that evening, Callum realised that making the 'nasty pasty' for Dad wasn't a very nice thing to do, as it tasted disgusting. He realised that he should never judge food by its appearance and he had found out that he loved real Cornish pasties after all!

"Dad's pasty really was nasty and the Cornish pasty was delicious!" Callum announced.

Later, Callum and Nanny Dawe sat down and had a cream tea together. "What goes first, Nanny? Cream or jam?" asked Callum curiously.

"Always the jam first and the cream on top, my 'ansum!" explained Nanny Dawe. "It's the Cornish way!" she smiled.

"What about the tea? Where does that go?" Callum asked himself.

"Tea?" Nanny replied with a puzzled expression. When she looked around, Callum had poured tea all over his scones, making such a mess!

"You said it's a cream tea, Nanny!" Callum cheekily replied.

"Oh Callum!"

"Can we make pasties for tea again soon?" Callum asked Nanny. "You can show me how to really make the perfect Cornish pasty!" Callum apologised to Nanny Dawe and to his dad. From that day to this, Callum has never made a nasty pasty again, especially not one with carrots inside!

Also available in the series:

'I Brushed My Teeth With Hair Gel!'

Printed in Poland
by Amazon Fulfillment
Poland Sp. z o.o., Wrocław